Dear Parent:
Your child's love of reading starts here!

Every child learns to read in a different way and at his or her own speed. You can help your young reader improve and become more confident by encouraging his or her own interests and abilities. You can also guide your child's spiritual development by reading stories with biblical values and Bible stories, like I Can Read! books published by Zonderkidz. From books your child reads with you to the first books he or she reads alone, there are I Can Read! books for every stage of reading:

SHARED READING
Basic language, word repetition, and whimsical illustrations, ideal for sharing with your emergent reader.

BEGINNING READING
Short sentences, familiar words, and simple concepts for children eager to read on their own.

READING WITH HELP
Engaging stories, longer sentences, and language play for developing readers.

READING ALONE
Complex plots, challenging vocabulary, and high-interest topics for the independent reader.

ADVANCED READING
Short paragraphs, chapters, and exciting themes for the perfect bridge to chapter books.

I Can Read! books have introduced children to the joy of reading since 1957. Featuring award-winning authors and illustrators and a fabulous cast of beloved characters, I Can Read! books set the standard for beginning readers.

A lifetime of discovery begins with the magical words **"I Can Read!"**

Visit www.icanread.com for information on enriching your child's reading experience.
Visit www.zonderkidz.com for more Zonderkidz I Can Read! titles.

Work at everything you do with all your heart.
Work as if you were working for the Lord.
—*Colossians 3:23*

www.zonderkidz.com

Zachary's Zoo
ISBN-10: 0-310-71466-4
ISBN-13: 978-0-310-71466-8
Copyright © 2000, 2007 by Nappaland Communications, Inc.
Illustrations copyright © 2000 by Lyn Boyer

Requests for information should be addressed to:
Zonderkidz, Grand Rapids, Michigan 49530

Library of Congress Cataloging-in-Publication Data

applied for

Art Direction: Jody Langley
Cover Design: Sarah Molegraaf

Printed in China

07 08 09 10 • 10 9 8 7 6 5 4 3 2 1

story by Mike and Amy Nappa
pictures by Lyn Boyer

My name is Zachary.

I'm a zookeeper.

It is my job

to take care of the animals.

Uh-oh, I hear the tiger.

It is time to let him out.

Easy, Tiger.

I'm coming to let you out.

Wait a minute!

What is that?

It's the bear!

There is only one thing to do …

Lie down!

Hey, Bear, get off me!

Okay, okay, I'll get your breakfast.

Stop licking me! It tickles!

I love taking care of God's animals.

I want to do my best.

That is how I say thank you to God for making me a zookeeper.

Oh no! The crocodile must be loose.

ZACHARY

Aha! I got you, Croc!

No need to worry, Mom.

I will save you.

It's not safe for you to be out.

You could get hurt.

I will take care of you.

SNAP

Hmmm.

Croc, do you hear something?

I didn't forget you, Sharky.

I will take care of you.

Here is your food for today.

Don't forget to thank God for it.

Oh no! The angry eagle is loose!

Don't attack me!

I don't have my zookeeper tools.

I don't need tools.

A good zookeeper can solve this.

I see why you are angry, Eagle.

Your cage is dirty.

I will change the paper.

Now, let's see.

What else do I need to do?

I put clean paper in the cage.

I washed my hands.

What did I forget?

Oh, yes …

ME!